HER NAME
was HOPE

HER NAME
was HOPE

Becca Hyatt

XULON PRESS

Xulon Press
2301 Lucien Way #415
Maitland, FL 32751
407.339.4217
www.xulonpress.com

Unless otherwise indicated, Scripture quotations taken from the King James Version (KJV) – *public domain.*

Printed in the United States of America.

ISBN-13: 978-1-54565-997-7

Early childhood, which spans the period
up to eight years of age, is critical for cognitive
social, emotional and physical development.
The years between ages six and fourteen are time of
important developmental advances that establish a
childs sense of identity.

HER NAME WAS HOPE

PROVERBS 13:12 HOPE deferred makes the heart sick, but when the desire cometh it is a tree of life.

Hope is a joyful expectation of the future, to believe that where you are going in life is better than where you have been.

Proverbs 22:6 Train up children in the right way, and when they are old, they will not depart from it.

She wanted so much to find love and favor in the eyes of her Father, but it never came. She had a tender loving heart, and was very kind. She would search for love in many men throughout her life.

She gave herself away over and over again, only to end up alone, hurt and empty. She gave others hope but was there hope for her?

PRELUDE

Such irony that her name was Hope! She would both love and hate that name all of her life. She would love it because many times hope would be all she had, and hate it because sometimes there seemed to be none. Maybe that is why her Mother gave her that name, realizing that she would need hope in order to survive. When in times of hopelessness, the determination to persevere would rise up inside, and become her strength. She felt so alone, even as young as two years old, she had to be the parent, not the child.

Chapter 1

HUMBLE BEGINNINGS

BORN IN 1954, just after World War II, to a seventeen-year-old girl who wanted to get married to get away from home, and a nineteen-year-old boy who was an alcoholic, was not a family made in heaven. She was a small little thing, with blonde hair and green eyes. She was born into a bad situation and life would be harder than she could ever imagine. Poor, uneducated, country people living in the deep south struggling to make a living. There were no paved roads in this part of the country. They lived in shacks on dirt roads with no indoor plumbing and very little in the way of furnishings. They were a family of humble beginnings.

Her Father was tall with dark brown hair, and was a very handsome man. He was a hard worker and well like by all who knew him, but he was an irate, abusive husband and Father. He was an avid hunter with many hunting dogs, and hunted squirrels, rabbit, birds and deer. The family ate from his spoils. He made his living as a logger, but they called it "pulp wooding", working with men who cut down trees in the woods. The work was hard, the weather harsh, and the days long. The trees were cut down with chainsaws, and loaded by hand onto trucks, which were then driven

to local sawmills and sold for mere pennies. They were then trimmed and sawed into lumber, and sold to building supply companies.

Mother was very pretty, with long black curly hair, and was blessed with a perfect figure. She had a winning personality and when she smiled it could make you shiver. Hope enjoyed watching her put on her makeup and the few beautiful dresses she had with her heels, and thought her mother was the most beautiful woman in the world. Hope wanted to look just like her someday.

As a small child Hope was taken to the woods and had to stay all day while her family worked. Times were hard, and the weather in the south was hot. There were no toys to play with, and you were not allowed to misbehave. Children were to be seen, not heard, so you had to be quiet and stay out of the way, or there would be consequences. Punishment would be a lashing with a stick cut from a bush in the woods. It would sting, burn, sometimes bleed, and leave whelps on your skin. Staying quiet was not easy for Hope because she loved to talk.

Hope was very mature for her age, and sadly, at the age of four she knew far more than most ten year olds would ever know. The local Baptist Church knew how bad things were for Hope and they sometimes stopped by and took her to Church on Sunday. She loved the Church, and she loved God. Something felt different there than what she felt at home. There was no anger there, and people seemed happy. They talked about love and Gods love. This is what Hope wanted for her family and herself. She wanted to be happy and loved.

Her father was an angry violent man, and if his hunting dogs did not perform to his liking, he would beat them and sometimes even kill them. He had so much hate and anger inside him, and she always wondered why.

Hope was only two years old when her sister was born and they named her Joy. She really was a joy to Father. Hope loved having a baby to enjoy as well. It gave her something to be happy about. She sang songs to Joy and held that sweet baby girl, just as though it were her very own. In some ways she would belong to her, and Hope was very protective of Joy. She was not jealous of the fact that Father loved Joy, but never seemed to love her. It was easy to love Joy, and it was not her fault that Dad chose not to love Hope.He never took a hand to Joy. His angry hands were always used against Hope and his wife when in his drunken rages.

Whether she was mature enough physically or emotionally, Hope had to care for her Mother and Joy when he was out of control. She took her job seriously, and could clean up all the bloody messes he made of her

Mothers' face to make it all better. Hope prayed a lot for God to change her Dad, and believed that someday that would happen.

Chapter 2

ONLY THE STRONG SURVIVE

MOTHER LIKED BEING with other men when Father wasn't around.

Who could blame her? There were many men in and out of the home when he was at work and he suspected as much, which made him drink more and lash out more. Everything seemed to revolve around alcohol. If he couldn't afford to buy it he would make it himself. He would also sell it to other "drunks" who would come by the house late at night, in order to make money. There was never a shortage of sloppy drunks around the house. He would even make Hope drink "moonshine" sometimes, and was amused at seeing her stumble around drunk and falling.

The physical abuse was so severe at times that he would put a knife to Mothers throat and threaten to slice it and Hope would have to plead with her Dad to drop the knife, while her Mother cried. There were severe beatings that would take place, leaving Mother bleeding and bruised. Hope would get wet cloths and gently wipe away the blood from her Mothers' face and try to console her. She was always begging for him to have mercy on her Mother. He seemed to enjoy the begging, and the pain he saw in their faces.

Mother had a cousin whose name was Lucy. She and Jim had five children. Jim was an alcoholic too and the couples spent a lot of time together because they both worked in the same business of logging. When they were together drinking bad things would always happen. Father and Jim would go out drinking, leaving their wives and children together at Lucy's home. One night, after they had been out drinking, they were followed home by two men they had a dispute with at a bar. The men followed them into the house and a bloody knife fight began Hope quickly gathered the children together and hid them behind the sofa in the living room where the fight was taking place.She was terribly frightened and began to pray. The other children were crying, and Hope whispered to them to be as quiet as possible as she tried to console them. It seemed like hours before the fight ended, but it was finally over and no one was killed. Mother and Lucy rushed out of the kitchen to find their husbands wounded and took them to the hospital.

Hope stayed behind with the children. Of course everything turned out to be okay, except for the fear pain inflicted on the children; not that they mattered. No one ever seemed to be concerned about the children. Their version of fun would always included alcohol, sex, and fighting. Hope hid all these things in her heart and tried to put it out of her mind. But for a young girl, these things are very hard to forget, and in reality, they stay in your heart forever.

As Hope and Joy grew, they lived in many different places. They never had an inside bathroom, but an outhouse in the backyard which was usually full of spiders and other insects, sometimes even snakes, which terrified

Hope. She still had no choice but to go to the outhouse alone, because no one cared. She learned at an early age not to count on anyone but herself and her maternal grandparents to survive in life, and that life was hard. In this world, you had to be tough, even when you felt weak, alone, and scared, because only the strong survive!

Chapter 3

SECRETS LOCKED
AWAY IN HER HEART

WHEN HOPE WAS five years old and Joy three years, they were playing outside with a small table and a little tea set when a man drove into the yard. He got out of his car, and walked onto the front porch where she and Joy were playing carrying a carton of chocolate milk. It startled Hope, but he seemed friendly enough.

Without speaking, he gave Hope the carton and, went inside the house. Mother was inside alone so this concerned Hope. She carefully opened the screen door, quietly creeping inside. Not seeing him or her mother anywhere, she heard a noise in the bedroom. Moving slowly to the door, she peeked through the keyhole and saw her mother in bed with him. Having heard and seen her parents in this act many times before, and the arguments over it as well, she knew what was going on, but was sad and disappointed for reasons she could not discern, and her heart sank. Such confusing information for a little girl to process. Hope had seen her mother kiss men before, but this had never happened.

Though her heart was sad, she quietly went back to her little party with Joy and tried hard not to think about the confusion in her head and the feelings in the heart.

She never wanted to trouble Joy with her burdens, and spoke not a word of the things she had seen to anyone. As usual, they were locked away in her mind and heart, along with all her other secrets.

Mother had started working as a waitress at a bar, which did not seem to bother Dad, because that gave him even more opportunities to stay out all night and get drunk, even though he was supposed to be taking care of Hope and Joy. But this would not keep him from doing what he liked most, so they would just have to accompany him by tagging along in the back seat of the car to his favorite bar where he would leave them while he drank himself into a daze. One rainy night Father decided he wanted to get drunk, so he drove to his favorite bar.. When he arrived they were given strict instructions to lie down in the back seat of the car and go to sleep. It was very cold that night and there were no blankets, so Hope held Joy close in order for them to try and stay warm. The doors were locked,the windows rolled up, and moisture was beginning to form on them. As they lay sleeping someone began knocking on the window. It startled Hope and she raised her little head, only to see two police officers looking in the window. She was terrified! They instructed her to roll down the window.

With trembling hands, Hope rolled the window down just enough to hear the police officer ask where her parents were. She told them her Father was inside the bar, but her Mother was at work. After asking what her Father's name was, they went inside the bar, made him come out and take them inside. Dad was told that he should never leave them in the car again or he would be arrested. Joy and Hope spent the rest of the night in that bar, which was nothing unusual for them. They spent a lot of time in bars, and even in the homes of strangers, while Dad was out drinking. Sometimes they would spend the night in the storage room of the bar where Mother worked, huddled in the corner. Dad was in the bar drunk and Mother was working.

Chapter 4

HAPPINESS SNATCHED AWAY

AT THE AGE of six Hope started to school. She was very excited, but sad that she had to leave Joy at home. Who would watch after her? Certainly not Mother. Riding the bus was a new and fun experience. Hope made a new friend the first day of school. Her name was Linda. She only wanted one friend, and did not want that friend to have any other friends except her. Hope was not good at sharing the people she loved with anyone else. She was very insecure and terrified of losing anyone that she loved. She was determined that absolutely no one would take her friend from her.

Linda walked home everyday for lunch.

One day Linda did not come back after having lunch at home, and Hope was terrified. This was not like Linda at all. The next day Linda was not at school, and the teacher announced that she had been hit by a car while crossing the highway. Hope was hurt beyond words. She began crying uncontrollably. The teacher took her out of the classroom trying to console her, telling Hope that Linda would be okay, and that she was alive. She said that Linda would be coming back to school after her recovery, but there was no consoling Hope. The principal actually had to take her to Linda's house so she could see with her own eyes that Linda was alive and would recover. Once Hope saw that Linda was going to be okay, she calmed down and went back to school. When Linda returned to school it made Hope very happy.

On one particular beautiful summer day Hope got off the school bus filled with excitement about the day she had at school. Her grades were excellent, the teacher liked her, and told her as much. Linda was back at school and they played together at recess every day. She ran into the house to show Mother the schoolwork she had brought home with her good grades, only to find that her father had Mother in the kitchen floor, on her knees with a knife at her throat. She was crying and begging him to let her go. He was pulling her head back by her hair and accusing her of having a boyfriend named Bill.

Hope knew that Mother had been seeing Bill because she and Joy had been in the car when they were together at times. Hope started crying and begging Dad to put the knife down, and he started yelling at her saying, "start praying to that God of yours that I don't cut her head off right now, start praying", so she began to pray. Then he said,"you tell me right now that she has been seeing Bill or I will cut her head off", and Hope said "no". She was afraid that if she said yes that Dad would kill her Mother.

But he held the knife even closer to Mothers' neck and she screamed louder. He yelled for Hope again to tell him that Mother had been meeting with Bill and so Hope said,"yes, yes, she has been seeing Bill, but they are just friends, and all they do is talk, please let her go, let her go, please". He let her go, while he cursed her, and Mother fell in the floor crying. while he left in a drunken rage. Hope held her Mother as she cried, and then looked for Joy. She found her under the bed, in their room crying, and comforted her

The happiness that Hope had felt that day about her achievements at school were quickly snatched away, as the terror of her life at home took over. Someday, Hope thought, our lives will be better, someday. But that day would not come the way Hope believed that it would.

Chapter 5

SHE WAS STRONG

One dark rainy night, things escalated to the most critical place Hope had ever witnessed. She had always been able to control the situation, but it was different this time. After a night of drinking at the bar where Mother worked as a waitress, Hope and Joy had been left in the stockroom, and Dad had gotten very drunk. When they finally got home, Hope put herself and Joy to bed in the room next to her parents.

They had not even gone to sleep before her Father started yelling profanity and chasing her mother down the hall, screaming at her that if she couldn't have sex with him she could spend the night outside in the rain. He locked her outside, on the front porch. Hope saw him coming back down the hall naked and falling into bed. She wanted to let her mother back in but knew she would have to wait until he was passed out, so she lay there in silence, listening for her father to start snoring.

Suddenly she heard the sound of the car door slam. Unfortunately, her Father heard it slam too, and he jumped out of bed, stormed down the hall, headed for the front door, and Hope knew what was coming. She tried to stop him from going outside, but he didn't even seem to notice her as he, stumbled down the hall in the dark. Now she had to focus on what to do next, so she ran into the room she shared with Joy, whispering in her ear to stay quiet, and pretend to be asleep.

Hope told Joy she was going to run to the neighbors and have them call grandmother, and not to tell anyone. She quietly crept out the back door into the darkest night she had ever known, went around to the side of the house, and watched as her Dad pulled her frightened mother out of the car. There were twelve concrete steps leading up to the front door. He held her by her long, dark curly hair, hitting her head on each step, as he pulled her by her arms up each one. Mother was crying, and begging hiim to stop but he was deaf to her words.

As soon as he had her inside Hope started running into that old muddy road, with the rain hitting her little face. Her tears were hot and the raindrops cold. Each drop of rain stung almost as much as her tears. She could hear dogs barking in the distance, and she was so afraid, but she had to be strong. She was strong! She ran as fast as she could to the nearest neighbors house and when she finally arrived at the nearest neighbors, Hope began desperately banging on their door. The lights came on, and they took her in, grabbing a blanket, they began to dry her cold, wet little body, as well as her tears. They calmed her down and listened to her little voice as she asked for them for help. Already having an idea of what was going on, but not wanting to get involved, they called her grandparents, who came right away and took her to their home. After hearing the details of that horrible night, Grandfather got into his car and drove off to try and get mother and Joy. Hope knew her father would not hurt Joy, butcouldn't count on him not hurting her mother, so she waited and prayed.

Only God knows how Mother managed to get away with her life that night, but Grandfather brought her to his home safe. Hope ran out of the house excited to see her Mother and sister, only to discover that Joy had been left behind. It crushed her to know that her sister was alone with Dad in his condition. They all climbed into Grandfathers car and drove back to the house to try and get Joy.

When they arrived, he was backing out of the driveway, with Joy in the car beside him. Horrified at the thought of him driving in his condition with her in the car, they followed him up the mountain, as he drove to his Mother's home. He was swerving from one side of the road to another, barely able to keep from running off the side of the mountain. Hope was terrified that he was going to kill himself and Joy. When he pulled into the dirt road at his Mother's house, he took Joy inside. Grandfather and Mother knocked on the door and Dads' Mother came out on the front porch and started yelling at them. They were asking her to let them have Joy, and she was not about to let her go with them. She always took up for her son, no matter what. Grandmother knew the only way they would get Joy back was to have Father arrested and that once he was in jail Mother could get her back.

In those days access to law enforcement and judges was very easy. Everyone knew everyone in this small little town. After a late night trip to the police and a visit to the judges' house in the middle of the night, Joy was reunited with Hope and her Mother.

Finally, Hope believed her future could be changing for the better.

Chapter 6

SCARRED FOR LIFE

AT THE AGE of seven, she went to live with her maternal grandparents. Her Mother took Joy to her cousin in Mississippi to prevent her Father from trying to snatch her. Hope had a plan. She believed they were all going to be happy. Once Mother got a divorce and it was safe to come back home, she could get a job and they could start a new life, just the three of them. Hope could help out around the house after school and Grandmother would watch Joy during the day. A perfect life. No alcohol or violence. Life could finally be healthy. But things in Hope's life would not be perfect or healthy. This would be the start of a new and dark chapter in both her and Joy's life. This one would leave them both scarred for life.

Hope would not see her mother and Joy for what seemed like a very long time, but in reality it was only a month. She did see her Father on occasion when he would pass Grandmother's home, but he never even bothered to turn his head and look her way, but one day he actually stopped, which terrified Hope. But it was only to tell Grandfather that he wanted nothing to do with Hope and that as far as he was concerned, she belonged to her grandparents. Grandfather took Hope into his arms and very boldly proclaimed to him that he would walk through hell barefoot for her, and would kill anyone who tried to hurt her or Joy. This made her feel wanted and loved, but at the same time, the rejection of her Father was like a knife in her heart. This should not come as a surprise to her, because she knew this already. But having it said out loud was quite another thing. That made it real. He had never said it out loud before, but now that he had, it was sealed in her heart forever, causing her even more emotional damage that would effect her relationships throughout her life in ways she could not imagine.

When Hope saw Mother mother again, she would be dropping Joy off, but not staying. She would be leaving them, and going back to stay with her cousin to work as a waitress in a cafe. Hope was thrilled to see her sister, but could not understand why Mother did not stay. Why not get a job here? They could be together as a family. Hope was prepared for not having Father in her life, but not having Mother was unthinkable. She had learned to accept a lot of things in her life, but could she accept this?.

At least she felt safe and loved here with her Grandparents, but Hope knew Mother would need someone to take care of her, and felt that she was the only one capable of doing that. Hope tried to put things out of her mind, but she always kept them in her heart.

Chapter 7

HOPE FELT LOVED

LIFE WITHOUT MOTHER was hard emotionally, and life with her Grandparent's was very hard in many ways. They were very poor and uneducated. Her grandfather had never even went to school. He was a tall man with a square face, and quite handsome. Grandmother had only went as far as the fourth grade and had been physically abused by her stepdad. She was in every way the grandmother, loving and caring. She sang as she worked and smiled often, even though she had very little, she appeared to be content. She was very pretty, with her light brown hair, and you could tell where Mother got her good looks from. Grandfather was nine years older than Grandmother and was a very quiet and passive man who seldom talked at all, but for the most part was only there. He worked at just about anything in order to support the family, and so did Grandmother. They worked hard and were good people.

They had to grow their own food and put it away for the winter. Pigs were raised and slaughtered in late fall by shooting them in the head with a rifle, skinning them, draining the blood, and then butchering them into various types of meats, which were packed in salt for preservation, then put in the smokehouse. Nothing was wasted, not even the brains, which Grandfather fried and ate with his eggs at breakfast, making Hope very sick. Everyone had to work, regardless of their age.

They even worked in other farmers fields as well, getting paid ten cents a bucket to pick tomatoes or beans, all while bending over in the hot fields all day long. Cotton was picked in late fall and put into a long bag, which was tied around your shoulder and dragged through the field until it was full. The cotton was picked from a hard round ball the size of a golf ball, called a burr, which popped open when it matured. It had sharp burrs at the top of it, almost like thorns, which would sometime stick your fingertips, causing them to bleed, getting blood on the beautiful white cotton. You had to pick with your back bent all day long and at night your back ached so bad it was hard to sleep.

Grandmother got up early every morning and cooked homemade biscuits and they were also carried for their lunch. On rare occasions, they would all climb into the back of a farmers pickup truck and would be driven to a local store and they got a coca cola and a candy bar! This was a divine pleasure for Hope and Joy! Their clothes were given to them by neighbors or sewn for them from scraps of material given to them. Even though the work was hard and they were poor, life was better living with her Grandparents. At least Hope felt loved.

Grandmother was angry with Grandfather most of the time. She yelled at him a lot, and made it no secret that her marriage to him was a mistake, and only a way out of her life with her step-dad, who was physically abusive to she and her three sisters. He was not abusive to the other nine children born to he and her Mother. Grandmother's siblings came around often and were usually drinking or drunk. Most of them had bad reputations for good reasons.Hope did not like being around them. Their language was as foul as their breath and she did not feel safe with them there.

Hope witnessed a lot of arguments between her Grandparents. Once she caught Grandmother with a broom in hand, chasing Grandfather around the kitchen table until she cornered him, and threatened to beat him with the broom. There always seemed be an argument about something, but there was never blood, knives, alcohol or guns, and as far as Hope was concerned, that was peaceful. But there was another secret in this home.

Grandmother often talked on the phone to the man that she confessed to having loved all her life. She did not keep this from Hope, Joy or her daughter, and it was well known that they were in love and would have married each other if he had not been in the military when Grandmother had to get away from her abusive situation at home. Marrying Grandfather was her way to accomplish that. In those days a woman could not get a job and take care of herself in society. Marrying and having children was the way out for women at that time.

There were times when on the way to buy necessities that suddenly Grandmother would pull the car over on the side of the highway and another car parked right behind her. It would be the love of her life. They would stand on the side of the highway and talk. Hope never saw them touch or kiss, unlike Mother and the men she met. But she told tales of Grandfather having being drunk in the past and her having to hunt him down and pull him out of bed with other women. These things appeared to be a normal way of life in Hope's family. She assumed these were normal things that happened in everyone's family. Hope wondered if there was a man or woman alive that was happy in their marriage.

Chapter 8

THE PEDDLER

HOPE'S GRANDMOTHER WANTED her to have a relationship with Father's family, even though there had been some bad blood in the past, so Hope and Joy spent the night with his Mother occasionally. She was a very tall and stocky woman, and very plain. She only wore old fashioned dresses and a bonnet. Her feet were huge and when she laughed her body shook all over. It made you laugh too. It was fun when they were there. They didn't have to work, and she would tell them "tales". They were usually "spooky tales", but nonetheless, it was much better than working in the crops. Granny's husband had been dead a long time and she had never re-married. Her hair was very long and she would braid it every morning and twist it around her head and pin it up. It was fascinating to watch.

There was to television to watch so she would take ashes from the fireplace, put them in a moist coffee cup and whirl it around. She would then turn it upside down and

23

let it get dry inside. Once it was dry she would take the cup that you chose and carefully look in the cup and read the condition of the ashes and tell your fortune. It was very entertaining to young girls. There were no stores close by to buy your food, and Granny did not farm. But there was a man who had transformed an old school bus into a traveling grocery store. He was called the "peddler". He would come by when Hope and Joy were there and they could go on the bus and buy candy and cans of soup. This was something out of a dream for them. They thought Granny was rich, even though she lived in a shack and had to draw her water from a well. They could pick out any candy they wanted and got Mary Jane chews, Banana Bike chews, Tiny Wax Soda Bottles filled with coulored liquids, and striped coconut bars.A can of Campbell's Chicken Noodle Soup was divine! They were in a heavenly place.

Granny was somewhat of a local celebrity. Many years ago Papa's family had settled the territory in the early eighteen hundreds and claimed one hundred and sixty acres in the state of Alabama. It was on a rocky mountain and in an area where there were rock formations. A man from Birmingham, Alabama came to the area and was fascinated by the rocks in the nineteen sixties and purchased the land with the rock formations and named it Horse Pen Forties. It was forty acres and he named each rock formation. It became quite famous and so did Granny. She baked her "Baptist Bisquits" at the festivals that were held there. Fanny Flag came there for promotion purposes and took pictures with Granny holding a shotgun, just for fun. Grandmother even cooked bisquits there sometimes. Granny appeared on the Tom York show in Birmingham, cooking her famous bisquits.

Father would drive by Grandmother's often and stop at the neighbors house. There was a woman he was seeing there. They would get drunk together and eventually had a son together. She was already married to someone else, so needless to say, the young boy grew up across the road from Hope and Joy as another man's son, but Hope knew that he was her brother. Father had always wanted a son. Now he had one but another man would raise him as his own. How sad and pitiful.

Eventually Father got married and had two daughters. They lived by Granny on the mountain and farmed. He was still drinking and was very abusive to his wife and children. Once he poured gasoline on her, and chased her through the field, trying to set her on fire. Another time when he was drunk, he got his gun, and was about to shoot her, and she ran to the car, started driving away and he shot at the car six times, leaving six bullet holes in the car to prove it. Luckily, she was not shot.

He would beat his oldest daughter often, and for no reason at all. She was a good girl but had a hard time because of him. There were many other stories told about him that made their way back to Hope, and she believed them all. She knew how awful things could be living with him and she empathised with her sisters, but did not understand the reason why his wife stayed with him. Hope knew in her heart that if she ever had children of her own, that they would never be abused by anyone, even their own Father.

Chapter 9

OH, SO MANY SECRETS!

NOT MUCH TIME had passed, and one summer day a car drove into the driveway. Mother got out of the car along with a man whose name was Bob. Hope and Joy were still in the one bedroom where they all slept, but as usual, Hope heard everything that was going on. When they entered the three room house Mother introduced Bob as her husband. Her HUSBAND? She had just gotten out of her marriage! Her HUSBAND! How could she even think about getting married again right now?

Grandmother (being the dominant one in her marriage) was LIVID!Her Grandparents took Mother outside to have a stern talk with her and while they were outside Bob went into the bedroom, which was in plain sight, and he thought the girls were sleeping. Hope pretended to be asleep as he pulled down her panties and looked at her, carefully examining her private parts. It lasted for only seconds, but she was terrified and couldn't move. She had been abused by her Father's angry hands, but was never touched like this before! This felt wrong, but she was scared to move! What should she do? Should she scream? Would he hurt her if she screamed? If he dared to touch Joy she would do whatever possible to protect her.

27

Suddenly the door opened and Grandmother was coming in the house, followed by Mother and Grandfather. Bob quickly slipped back into the other room before they saw him. Grandmother had given her daughter a good tongue lashing for having gotten married thirty days after her divorce. Mother wasn't happy about it at all, and was going to take the girls and leave with Bob. But Grandmother was not about to let the girls go anywhere with a stranger, and Hope was very happy about that decision. So Mother drove away that day and would not return for a long time. Hope hid yet another secret in her heart. Oh, so many secrets!

Chapter 10

POOR, WHITE TRASH

HOPE EXCELLED IN school, pleasing her grandmother and her teachers but Joy just couldn't make good grades and impress her teachers or Grandmother somehow. Joy was petite and pretty, but Hope was chubby, and not very pretty. She did everything possible to make up for being ugly and fat, using her gift to make Grandmother laugh even when she was mad. That was one of Hope's best assets.

Grandmother wanted Hope to take piano lessons and learn to play the piano, so her grandmother worked for the neighbor, cleaning out their chicken house after the chickens had been taken to the slaughter, in order to buy a used piano for Hope. A teacher at the school where Hope attended gave her lessons after school one day a week. This teacher took a special interest in Hope, and the feeling was mutual. She learned to play right away, and soon played, as well as sang, in Church to make her grandmother happy. It became imperative for her to please the people in her life who were kind to her and showed her attention, not realizing this would turn out to be a bad thing for her in the future. Grandmother bought a used piano with the money she had earned and Hope learned to play.

Joy was always liked by the boys and wasn't interested in music. She only wanted a horse, and not a piano. She was very much the tomboy. She missed Father and needed a father figure in her life, someone who would take her fishing or hunting. If someone like this ever came into her life she would do almost anything to please him, which would cause her much pain. Joy was the total opposite of Hope. She was quiet and reserved around grown ups, and had very few friends that were girls. Her friends were mostly boys, and this would be a pattern throughout her life. She enjoyed fishing and hunting, but Hope loved being a girly girl, even though she was not attractive.

The boys on the school bus made fun of Hope, calling her fatty, and big nose. It hurt, but she didn't cry in front of them. But when her feet stepped off that bus the tears started flowing, and she would run into the house into her grandmothers' loving arms, where she would be comforted. There was always something cooked, and ready to eat everyday in Grandmother's kitchen. Food was a source of comfort for Hope, and Grandmother was a wonderful cook.

Grandmother was a strict disciplinarian, and if you disrespected her you would receive punishment by receiving lashes, with what she called a 'hickory'. It was a small limb from a bush that you, and you alone, had to cut When Hope was thirteen, she started getting smart with her grandmother and on one occasion, Hope had talked back to Grandmother, and had to cut a 'hickory'. When receiving the stripes. they seemed especially harsh, causing Hope to wonder why this lashing seemed to come from such anger, making her sad. This hurt her emotinally, making her feel unloved at the time.

The following day she was dressing in her gym clothes at school and heard the other girls gasping. She looked around to see what was going on and they were staring straight at her, and not knowing what was going on, Hope quickly covered herself. When she asked what they were looking at, they questioned her about her back. She explained that she was disrespectful to her grandmother, and had received a whipping. Hope asked if they did not receive that kind of punishment from their parents when they were disrespectful, and they quickly told her this was abuse, not punishment, and they had never had that happen to them! Hope knew all too well what abuse was, or at least she thought she did, but it made her feel different, ebarrassed, and only reinforced what she already knew in her heart. Her life was, and always would be "different" than that of the other girls.

Their parents were not divorced, and they went to Church every Sunday. They were well known in the community, well-liked, and every Mother, except hers, attended school functions. Hope knew people whispered about her and her family behind their back, "poor white trash". Sometimes she felt that it was true, never feeling accepted, or good enough, and unable to participate in the activities at school. She was different than everyone else, and that made her sad, lonely, and hurt.

The neighbors had two boys. One was the same age as Joy, and his brother Tom was a few years older than Hope. They played with the younger boy whenever possible, but didn't have a lot of free time, because they were always busy working. Hope was having some trouble with math in school, and grandmother suggested she go next door to have Tom help her. Tom agreed and one day while they were at his dining room table, going over her math problems, she suddenly felt something moving up her leg. She looked under the table, and saw his hand moving up her leg headed in a direction it should not be going, and she jumped up from the table, grabbed her books, then ran out of the house crying. Once again, someone had tried to take advantage of her and it felt dirty. She never told her grandmother what happened, and never went back there when Tom was home. What was it with men anyway. She was fat, she was ugly, so why did this happen to her? Maybe it was true, maybe she was just poor white trash.

Grandmother often took Hope to visit her Father's family. While out outside playing with her cousins on one Sunday afternoon, having a carefree time, one of the boys chased her into an outbuilding. She thought it was just part of the game and ran inside, thinking nothing of it. He closed the door, unzipped his pants, and exposed himself to her. As he started walking toward Hope, she screamed loudly, and her Aunt came running to her rescue. He was quickly beaten with a stick from the yard by his mother.

Hope stopped playing with the other kids that day. She felt dirty and sad inside. White trash, just pure white trash. What she heard folks whisper behind her family's back had to be true, and this just proved it.

Chapter 11

MOTHER CAME BACK

WHEN **H**OPE **WAS** fourteen years old her mother came back into her life, and when she did, there was a new baby. A healthy, adopted baby boy. They had wanted to have children, but having failed to conceive, they had adopted a baby boy. Hope became very jealous and angry. Mother had left her own two children behind and made a new family for herself. She felt betrayed, and did not understand how her mother could desert her own children, adopt a child who belonged to someone else, and choose Bob over them. It caused Hope to hate the baby before she even saw him, and she tried very hard not to love him. But Hope's heart was much bigger than she even knew. There was no room for hate in her heart. Once she saw that baby, she fell in love with him. His name was Rob, and he was a chubby little angel!

Mother started spending money to buy Hope and Joy gifts at Christmas, and they got new clothes. They no longer had to wear hand me down clothes, which was wonderful. Hope decided to put the nasty things behind her and accept Bob. She and Joy began to go and spend the summer months with Mother and Bob. Hope didn't like Bob, and saw that he was controlling and hateful. But Mother loved Bob more than anything in the world. Much more than she loved her children, and that would become even more obvious as the years went by.

When Hope was sixteen years old Mother gave birth to a baby girl,and that is just what Bob wanted, a little girl! Hope was excited about having a baby sister, and Mother even let Hope pick the name for the baby girl. Her name was Grace. She was a beautiful baby, and both Hope and Joy adored Grace. They went to stay with Mother after Grace was born, so they could help with things around the house. Bob was actually on his best behavior, and he was very happy about having a baby girl. Hope even got a work permit so that she could work in a retail store, and that made her feel so grown up! She was not used to having a job like this. The work was easy compared to working in the fields back home. Mother let her drive her car to work, and Hope made a friend there. She bought some some new clothes for the new school year which would be starting in a few months. Hope did not give her customers or co-workers a big smile, because her front teeth had cavities, and she was embarrassed. They had no insurance, and could only go to the dentist when a tooth got so bad that it had to be pulled.

Hope would be starting the tenth grade this coming year, and wanted so badly to get her teeth filled, but knew that it would not happen, so she just gave her customers a smile with her mouth closed. but she was still the happiest girl at that store.

Chapter 12

WHAT IS WRONG WITH HER?

HOPE'S FATHER HAD finally seemed to settle down, and was drinking less. He had gotten a job in a factory because his farming business was not doing well and had dental insurance at this job which would cover his children. When Grandmother heard about this she insisted he add Hope and Joy to his insurance, because he had never done much in the way of supporting them.

Father knew he had failed when it came to helping his children born from his first marriage. and Grandmother was quite convincing when she wanted something done. When Hope found out she was so excited that her prayers were finally answered. New clothes for the school, and her teeth would be pretty! She would feel good about herself now!

Her step-mother picked her up from school one afternoon and they drove to the dentist office. That was one of the most exciting days of Hope's life. The smile she gave her classmates the next day was big, beautiful, and confident. Things were looking up for Hope.

She was in the tenth grade this year, and made a new friend right away. Her name was Jill. Grandmother let her spend the night with Jill quite often. Her Dad was a Pastor at a local Church, and their family were very decent people. Hope had never been on a vacation, and did not even know what that meant, other than what she had heard. Jill's family invited her to go to the beach with them on vacation, and Grandmother let her go. She even bought her a swim suit, which was something that Hope had never been allowed to have before. She had never even worn shorts, much less a swimsuit. Hope was never allowed to go swimming, and did not know how to swim, but was so excited about going on this trip with Jill and her family. She saw the ocean for the first time at the age of seventeen. It was breathtakingly beautiful! Hope would only put her feet in the water, as the waves washed over them. It was as frightening as it was beautiful, and was an experience of a lifetime.

As Hope and Joy grew up and became old enough to date, it became clear that grandmother was very strict and dating would be very controlled. Grandmother wanted her to date, Tom. She wanted nothing to do with him. It was impossible to meet boys because all Hope did was work, go to school and Church. But one day at the grocery store a young man who was working in the meat department started flirting with Hope, and it shocked her. She went home that day and dreamed about him that night.

Each time they went grocery shopping they talked, and finally Grandmother let her go out with him. On her first date, Hope had her first kiss, and it felt good in a way, but it also felt dirty. After a few dates he climbed on top of her and rubbed himself on her and she was disgusted and horrified! This made her feel so dirty! What is wrong with her? Why does this seem to happen to her every time she is around a man? She made him stop and take her home immediately.

With her being upset, Grandmother noticed it right away, and informed her that she couldn't go out with him anymore. He decided that he would get back at Hope and told two neighbor boys that he "made out" with Hope. On the school bus the next day the boys started making fun of her, telling everyone on the bus that she had "made out" with a boy. She got real upset and embarrassed. Of course she denied it. When she got home and told her Grandmother what he had done, she called him on the phone asking him to come over.

When he got there Grandmother asked him if he had sex with Hope. He admitted that they had not had sex. When she asked why he had told the neighbor boys what he did, he said he just wanted to brag. Grandmother put the fear of God in him and made him take Hope to the boys house and tell them he had lied, and apologize, as Hope, stood there listening. Their relationship was over, and now dating was impossible.

Chapter 13

A MARRIAGE MADE IN HELL

MOTHER AND STEP-DAD had moved back to town. They were always moving from place to place, and so At the age of severteen Hope decided it was time to move in with them because she wanted some freedom, and where she went Joy would always follow. They had an inside bathroom with a shower, and Hope could have her own bedroom, which was something she had always dreamed of having. She had long since let go of the past and knew it was not good to hold grudges anyway. If Hope had learned anything, it was that holding on to the past only made one cold, and she never wanted to be like the people in her life who were cold, bitter and unhappy. So at the age of seventeen, with Joy right behind her, they moved in with Mother.

Hope babysat after school, so her mother could go to work. Things were okay for a while. Hope was allowed to use the car on weekends, and cruise downtown with her friends. She met a guy who had just come home from the Vietnam war. All her life she longed to meet someone to love, who would love her in return. Someone who would give her a good life, a good home, and a family. That is all she ever wanted. His name was John, and he was four years older that Hope.

John was of average height and build. He had light brown hair, brown eyes, and was rather attractive, but was from a large, poor, and troubled family. Having five brothers and six sisters made it hard for his parents to make time for their children. In fact, the older children (of which he was the third oldest) were shown no love. It is hard to give love when you have not known love, and hard to have hope when you've had little hope.

Both parents had to work in order to feed their large family, and the kids had to work as well. They also had to grow their own food and put it away for the winter. Needless to say that family was starved for affection, much like Hope had been, but she was too blind to see that at the time.

John liked to drink, and that did bother her, but she accepted it, and on occasion would drink with him and his friends. At least he didn't get violent, which is something that made her feel good. She believed this was the man she would spend her life with and made her very happy. She could make a happy life with someone if they would just give her a chance.

One day when getting out of the shower she realized that someone was in the room watching her. It was Bob staring at her, so she screamed, wrapped herself in the towel, and he fled the room. Hope went to her room and stayed there until her mother came home. As soon as Mother came home, she told her what had happened. Bob was right there when she was telling Mother, and of course called her a liar. Mother believed him!

Hope called John, and was crying. She didn't tell him why at the time, but asked him to pick her up, that she had to leave home and would be walking up the highway. He drove from the next town and picked her up. After telling him what had happened, she begged him to let her live with him and his roommate, but was told no. Hope was a virgin, and was willing to sleep with John in exchange for a place to live. Never did it occur to her to go back to live with Grandmother (who had built an inside bathroom in her home to try and get Hope to come back). John told her that she would have to finish her senior year in high school before they could be together, and that he would then marry her. She was happy to hear that he would marry her, but at the same time her heart was broken. She thought he would help her. What would she do now?

Feeling that her only choice was to go back to her Mothers and finish school, she allowed John to take her back there. She chose to believe that she would marry him, and her life would be better. Three days before she graduated from high school, Hope and John were married in the home of a Preacher that Hope's family had known for years. They rented a three room apartment, attached to the home of a nice elderly couple, and Hope took to them right away.

The marriage for John was about control and sex. The marriage for Hope was about security and love. Another marriage made in hell.

Chapter 14

HER NAME WAS CHARITY

JOHN INSISTED THAT Hope work outside the home. The women in his family worked, and no wife of his would stay home. So Hope had to find a job and go to work. She found work at a local drug store as a cashier. Since they had only one car, she walked to work. It was in walking distance for her, so it wasn't a big deal during the summer, but in winter, or on rainy days it was difficult. Her mother loaned her a car because John refused to allow Hope to use his car. John was angry about the fact that she had a car, but it was tolerated for a time. One snowy day after finishing a shift at work, she discovered the car had a flat tire.

Since she had never changed a tire before, she walked home and asked John to come change the tire. He blew her off, and told her to change her own damn tire. She left the apartment crying, walked back to the car, and began the task of trying to change a flat tire. A man stopped to help her about the same time that John showed up, and started cursing at her. The man left, and John changed the tire while cursing and accusing Hope of having a boyfriend. There was no truth to his accusations and it reminded her of her father. There was no trust in the marriage. John was jealous of Hope, but he was not affectionate, and she needed affection desperately.

Hope began to beg John to let her get pregnant. She wanted a baby so bad. She wanted to be a Mother, a good Mother. He fought her about it for two years. but when she was nineteen he said yes. She stopped taking birth control pills and got pregnant within a few months. This was a happy time for her, even though John didn't feel the same way.

While at work one day she started bleeding, and went to the doctor, who was close by. He put her on bed rest for two weeks. She quit her job and stayed home per the doctors instructions, and they drifted further apart. He seemed to be in his own world these days, and she felt lonely and left out. Even though she still loved him, she realized that he could not give her what she needed. He didn't make her feel needed, loved, important or safe. Would anyone ever make her feel that way? She felt sure that her baby would make her feel that way. And she would give her baby all the love in her heart. Her baby would never feel unloved, unwanted, scared or alone. She would make sure of that.

They bought a small home and had very little in the way of furniture or anything else, but Hope was happy. John worked at a local factory whose manager was an acquaintance of Hope's family. She had contacted this man and pleaded with him to give John a job at the factory. John was hired there as an errand man. His job was to go to various places and pick up things for the maintenance department, run errands, and getting the mail from the post office. The baby came soon after the move. Her name was Charity. She was a beautiful baby with a head full of dark black hair that would later become blonde. Her eyes were brown and her cheeks were chubby just like her little legs. She was everything a mother could hope for and more. Hope had never been this happy!

Chapter 15

HIS NAME WAS BILL

Hᴏᴘᴇ ᴡᴏᴜʟᴅ ʙᴇ a stay at home Mom. Her dream had come true, most of it anyway. John started to technical school at night, and was gone most of the time. He barely spoke to Hope, and had nothing to do with the baby., de`-ja`vu!. Sounds somewhat similar to the marriage of her own parents.

Charity was what Hope woke up for every day, but she had gained a lot of weight, and she had to admit to herself that she was very unattractive. She started getting phone calls from her girlfriends telling her that John was coming by their home during the day asking for a glass of water and once inside he became sexually aggressive with them and they made him leave. They asked her to please tell him to stop. This news was very upsetting to her. When confronting John about it he brushed it off and made it seem as though they were trying to cause trouble for him, and that they had taken him the wrong way. Hope lost some friends because of this because she believed John, but there was still a voice in her head telling her that it could be true. After all, didn't men have a pattern of bad behavior. But so did women, and they would lie about it too. There were always two sides. She would try to hang onto her marriage. No one else would want her.

She was fat and ugly. Never once did Hope think of being unfaithful to her husband.

Joy was dating someone and found out she was pregnant, and they decided to get married. Hope went with Joy to give their grandmother the news. Grandmother became very upset, started to cry, and asked Joy why she couldn't have waited like Hope did, until the wedding night, to "be with her man". Hope spoke up at that time, informing her grandmother that she had not been a virgin on her wedding night either, and that was really upsetting for Grandmother. The things she learned that day were hard for her to process, but in time all was forgiven. Joy got married and had a beautiful baby girl, and they started spending time together.

Joy had gained weigh too, and they started a diet together. Hope looked, and felt like a new woman after losing the weight. She didn't look ugly anymore, but in her heart she would always be that fat, ugly, unlovable little girl that her Father never loved, and probably no man would ever truly love. But Hope started getting attention from men in a way she never had, and it felt good. She had watched it happen for Joy and her Mother many times, but had never experienced it herself. When a man would tell her how pretty she was, it was like winning the lottery! She drank it in like a glass of cool water. It felt so good to hear that said to her! After all the years of feeling like ugly, fat, white trash, it would only take a few sweet words to make her give herself away to a man she barely knew. What did she know of love? She longed to be held in a man's arms and feel safe. John had never made her feel loved. He was incapable of doing so. She needed that so badly, and had all her life.

What little Hope knew about love, she had learned by watching her parents, grandparents, and step-parents.

She would feel the feeling of being in love with any man who held her in their arms, told her they loved her and made her feel that they really did. So down the twisted path of deceit she went, following right along in the footsteps of her parents, somewhere she had sworn to herself she would never go. Aside from the guilt, feeling loved was one of the best feelings she had ever had. So she locked the guilt away in her heart along with all her other secrets, and went on with her affairs.

There was one man in particular that Hope was seeing. His name was Bill. He had served in the military but had just been released from duty and was looking for work. They met at a party and he took an interest in Hope. Having struck up a conversation, he asked for her phone number and she gave it to him because she was flattered that anyone was interested in her. John certainly didn't seem to care about her anymore. After talking on the phone a few times he came to Hope's home while John was not there; which was most of the time.

They were together from time to time, and really cared for each other. He told her was not happy in his marriage, and they talked about being together as a couple someday. But when John saw this change in her, he became interested in her and seemed to like the person she had become. He pursued her, and they were intimate (not that she was interested, because she wasn't, but it was her obligation).

On New Years Day she was helping her Mother cook, and felt something move within her. Hope instinctively knew what it was. She was pregnant! How could this have happened? Protection was used, and this was not in her plans.

Chapter 16

OTHER DARK SECRETS

W HEN H OPE WAS about seven months pregnant a man
came to the door and identified himself as a State Auditor.
He said he was there to asses the home and property for
tax purposes and that he would also need to come inside
the home as well. Being familiar with how this process
was normally done, Hope asked him for his ID, and he
produced it. It was totally legitimate so she let him in the
house after he had surveyed the outside area.

Charity was playing alone in the other room. He
grabbed her and told her that he had a "thing" for pregnant women and that he loved her long blonde hair. He
pressed his lips against hers and she was very frightened.
There were only four rooms in the home and they were
standing in plain sight of one bedroom. He pushed her
toward the bed, then shoved her down onto it and was
on top of her.

She did not fight back because of Charity. There was
no way she would traumatize her sweet little two year old
by screaming or making any noise at all. She lay there
and let him rape her while praying that the baby she was
carrying inside her would not be harmed in any way at all.

When he was finished, he got up, pulled up his trou-
sers, buckled his belt and informed her that she had

better keep her mouth shut, that if she told anyone they would not believe her because he was an important man with an important job, and that she was a nobody. She had no intention of telling anyone. She just wanted him to leave, and she would hide it in her heart with all her other dark secrets.

Two months later she gave birth to a beautiful baby daughter. She was so tiny and fragile, with a small bit of red hair and dark eyes. Her name would be Faith. Hope tried to have faith that things could work out with John. John loved Faith so much. She looked so much like him. It was uncanny how he loved her but didn't seem to care for Charity. How familiar that was. This hurt Charity as the years went by, and Hope tried her very best to compensate for the lack of affection her oldest daughter did not get from her father, but she knew all to well how painful it was.

When Joy was visiting one day and the girls were out playing, a big secret was revealed to Hope. John had tried to rape Joy when she was sixteen and had come to stay with them. She had fled after Mother's husband had done something bad to her. Hope remembered the day Joy left her apartment to go back home to Mother's and had always wondered why she left. And that wasn't all. When she was pregnant with her own daughter, John had gone by her apartment one day and tried to force himself on her, leaving her bruised and very upset. She fought him off, but never told anyone until now. Well that certainly got Hope's attention, and she finally saw John for who he really was. Now she had to make a decision.

Hope told John she was filing for divorce and he became very angry. He shoved her onto the floor and got on top of her, telling her she could not provide for herself and would never have anything. This did not scare Hope. Something rose up inside her that she had never felt before

Suddenly she felt empowered and would prove to him just how capable she was and that he was the one who would end up with nothing. After all, it was her who handled all the finances. He didn't know one thing about how to handle money. She would show him!

Chapter 17

HIS NAME WAS PAUL

SHE DIDN'T HAVE a car, and had to walk to the store for things she needed. Charity was in the first grade at school and rode the school bus. Faith was only three years old. The judge finally ordered John to provide Hope with a car, and she got a good job.

Grandmother cared for the girls while Hope worked.

Hope had joined a PTA bowling league and met a man who had worked with John. They struck up a conversation after a game on day, and it was revealed to Hope that John had been seeing a woman at the plant where he worked with this man. His name was Paul. Paul was not especially attractive, but he was very attentive to Hope, and there was something very tender and warm in his eyes when he looked at her. They began to see each other at the bowling alley every week and before long they found themselves in each others arms, kissing and longing for love from each other. Needless to say Hope fell head over heels in love with Paul, and he felt the same way about her.

John got married as soon as he could. He married a the woman he worked with at the plant, which was no surprise. The girls visited him sometimes, but did not like going there. Paul spent Christmas with Hope and her girls, but before leaving he told Hope that he was married with two daughter of his own and that he could not find it in his heart to leave his wife and daughters. Hope was devastated! Her heart had never been so broken. He left her that day and she thought she would absolutely die! In fact she tried to do just that. She fould every bottle of pills she could and swallowed them down, as her sweet babies lay in the next room. As she started to go to sleep she thought about her children and called Joy and ask her to come and get them and care for them. After questioning Hope, Joy drove to her house, gathered up the girls, Hope, and drove to the emergency room. Hope did not get to escape from her pain.

Soon the heartache turned into anger. How could he do this to her? Did he deserve to be happy while she lay here empty and broken? No! Vengeance had never been in her heart before, but it was now and she was unable to control her anger and called his home one night. His wife answered the phone, and she told her everything, then asked to speak to Paul. She put him on the phone, and Hope made him tell say he loved her on the phone, while his wife listened, but they stayed together in spite of it. She had never felt such anger and betrayal before. Once again she had been abandoned, betrayed, and hurt by yet another man. Would she ever stop hoping for love and just give up altogether?

Chapter 18

HIS NAME WAS JIM

JOHN HAD JUST gotten a divorce. His wife was pregnant with another mans baby, and had left him. Hope was at a bar one night and she ran into him. He sat down at her table, and they ended up going home together. What was she thinking? Was she crazy? Maybe the two of them deserved each other! Maybe it was because her Grandmother, who was keeping her kids for her to work, begged her to take John back. She kept telling Hope that the only thing important in a husband was that he was a good provider and that nothing else was important. As long as he doesn't beat you it's okay, she said. In a way that made sense. Her grandmother had never been provided for by her own husband. He was uneducated and unable to provide for her, leaving her to be the one who had to scramble to make a meager living for her family.

Eventually Hope took John back, but did not marry him at that time. She told her grandmother that they were married in order to make her happy, and it did. She had become weak and she knew it. What difference did it make anyway. She had lost the love of her life and nothing would ever be right again. If she couldn't have Paul she may as well just settle for John.

Hope decided to concentrate of the things she could do right. She bought her Grandmother a diamond cluster. and wedding band because she had never had a wedding ring. It made Hope happy to see her Grandmother who had sacrificed so much in life to raise her children and grandchildren, happy. She did this because she loved her grandmother, and appreciated the love and care she had shown her throughout the years. Happiness was not in the cards, but she would try and make it work. The job she had was very good and so was the money. John liked that part.

When Hope received her income tax refund she bought a washer and dryer for her grandmother, who had never owned one. She called to tell her that there would be a new washer and dryer delivered to her house the next morning, and found out that she was very sick. Later that night the phone rang, and Hope was told that her grandmother had been rushed to the hospital with a heart attack in critical condition.

She rushed to the emergency room as fast as she could. The family waited anxiously in the waiting room for hours, when finally the doctor came to tell them that she had died. Hope screamed as though someone were stabbing her heart. She felt as though someone had taken her heart and ripped it into a million pieces! How could God let this happen? This woman was the only person in her life that had ever loved her and been kind to her. She taught her about having proper credit, being a good mother and making her own kids feel safe. What would Hope do without her grandmother? And Hope had been lying to her, claiming to be married to John. This made her feel very guilty, and she would not live with this lie any longer. She would marry John and make her grandmother happy. That was the last thing Hope could do for her.

They went to the courthouse and got married. Faith stood against the wall and cried, and Hope was crying too. She cried so much that saying "I will" was almost impossible, but she managed to get the words out. They went to Church that next Sunday, along with the rest of the family. That would make her grandmother happy too.

Both John and Hope got involved in the Church for three years. She taught a Sunday School Class, and played the piano. Things were good for a time. Hope's Mother quit her job to take care of Grandfather, who was suffering from dementia, which drew Hope closer to her Mother. Her father became active in her life and he had finally settled down. But it was too little, too late. He had cancer and would suffer with it for four years before he lost his battle with it.

On his death bed Hope's Father told her he was sorry for all he had done to hurt her, and he begged her forgiveness. He was a sick, scared and weak old man. Hope cried with him and forgave him that day as he lay dying. At his funeral she and Joy weren't even allowed to sit with the family. They were shunned, and even sent thank you cards from his "family" for the flowers. More rejection, but this time it wasn't from her Father at least. It wasn't long before Grandfather died and was laid to rest beside Grandmother at the little country Church near the old home they shared.

Just as she knew it would, the marriage ended when Hope realized that if she must work and do everything around the house, raise the kids and be a sex slave for John at bedtime, then what was she doing in this marriage anyway? Why did she need him? She didn't! Her grandmother was wrong! She was gone and this was not making anyone happy.

John was so hard on Charity that she had threatened to run away if Hope stayed with him. And Hope had already found her a new man. His name was Jim. He was five years younger than her and very attractive. Jim had dark hair with a winning smile and personality, but later on she would find out things about him that she wouldn't like at all.

While Faith was with her Mother, Hope and Charity moved out of the house with John into an apartment when John was at work. John had no idea until he came home that day that his family had left him. Faith also had no idea she was about to be taken from her Dad. When Hope brought Faith home, and she found out about the divorce, with new living arrangements. she was very unhappy! But the three of them managed to start a new life together, and soon Jim was moving in with them. Faith and Charity took up with him right away. Everything seemed to be okay, but Hope had told them that she and Jim were married. She even showed them a fake marriage certificate. Of course, they told John their Mother had remarried, and there was nothing John could do but accept it, and so the lie became real for a while.

Chapter 19

HIS NAME WAS BRAD

HOPE FOUND A wonderful job with great benefits at a plant near her apartment, and the girls could walk to school. John remarried right away, of course. He was determined to make things hard on Hope and he managed to get get his child support lowered to a very low amount, and even then the checks would bounce. When Hope reported this to the court system he became disabled at his job, his wife left him and took everything he had. He came to the plant where Hope worked, cursing and blaming her for everything. When she heard him yell that he could no longer pay child support she told him to get his lawyer to draw up the papers saying he had to pay zero child support, that she would provide her children with everything they needed, his anger increased and he told her that she had always loved her children more than him anyway, to which she replied, " I sure did". He drove away that day, had the papers drawn up and Hope signed them.

Hope and a friend planned a vacation together with their families. They would all go to the beach for the weekend. Once at the beach, the girls decided they wanted to go to an amusement park. The adults wanted to drop the kids off at the park and leave them, but Hope would not drop her daughters off at an amusement park and leave them, so she took the girls and stayed with them at the park until they were ready to leave. It was too dangerous to leave young girls alone.

Anything could happen to them. She would always protect her daughters. Always! She was not like her mother. Upon returning to the condo, Hope found the adults all drunk and was told that her friend had sex with her boyfriend, as well as Jim. Whether that was true or not, that was the end of her relationship with Jim! Another disgusting man! Faith was disappointed! Especially when Hope told them she wouldn't have to get divorced because they were never married in the first place! Honestly, sometimes she could be so brutally honest! But there was already another man in her sites! His name was Brad.

Brad was fifteen years older than Hope and a supervisor at the factory where she worked as the office secretary. He was average in build, with dark hair, and wore glasses. He had a contagious laugh, and was always smiling. Brad wasn't necessarily attractive as far as looks, but he carried himself well and was very mature, settled, and educated. He lathered Hope with compliments, gifts, and brought her candy and sweet tea from her favorite lunch spots. He was really spoiling her, and she was enjoying it. She had no intention of getting involved with him, but he was very persistent.

In time Hope began to enjoy his advances and even gave in to him coming to her apartment one day. He kissed her like she hadn't been kissed in a very long time. She felt it all the way to her toes. There was only one problem, he was married. She tried to resist his charm, but of course needed the attention. She had been down this road before. Why did she have no self control? The feelings were so intense and exciting. He was very good to her. She quickly fell in love with him and he with her. They were together every moment they possibly could be.

Hope became quite the asset to her company, and was quickly promoted to a supervisory position, on the condition that she attend college, and get a two-year business degree. She gladly accepted the challenge and plunged into her new opportunity at work. She excelled in college, and in her career. She bought her first home and moved from the apartments into it with her daughters. This was on of the happiest days of her life. She had accomplished something at that time which was unheard of for a woman. The lady who closed the loan even bought flowers for the occasion, telling Hope how proud she was of her that day. Her career was going well, and her finances seemed to be great. Everything in her life was good, except her love life.

Hope had reached a point in her relationship with Brad in which she realized he would have to choose between her or his wife. This affair had been going on for five years, and she had done everything possible to get him to make a choice, even dating other men, and flaunting it right in front of him. She had suffered such depression over these years, and at times was unable to get out of bed or even work at times. Her friends and daughters were concerned about her. They tried to convince her to leave him alone, but she couldn't. Faith was very angry at her for seeing Brad because he was a married man. It took such a toll on her mind that she started seeing a therapist. He diagnosed her with bipolar depression disorder, and put her on medication. Because the therapist was concerned about her harming herself, he placed her in a mental health center for two weeks.

The girls were self-sufficient, and her insurance would cover the expenses, so she took advantage of this time to focus on her mental health. While at this retreat, she met a man nine years younger, who was there to help himself get off drugs, and turn his life around. He was a down to earth country boy, and very friendly to Hope. His name was David. They quickly became friends, and soon became inseparable. Upon her release, Hope invited him to move in with her, and he did. She was not in love with David, but was sympathetic towards him. He had never known his father, and had grown up in a community shunned because of that. Hope knew how it felt to be thought of as "white trash", and wanted to help him out because his mother was gone and he had nowhere to go. There was another reason for letting him move in with her too. She could use him to make Brad jealous, and maybe he would leave his wife so they could finally be together. But when her plan didn't work by moving David in, Hope got so angry that she married David. Finally, this would be her way of getting over Brad. Now that she was married to someone else, maybe he would leave her alone, and she could start a new life.

The girls got along great with David, and he fit right in. He got a job, and Hope bought him a brand new car. Everything seemed to be going well. Two years into the marriage Hope realized she had made a mistake. David was fired from his job, and accused of stealing money from the company. He lied to her about it at first, but ultimately confessed. David was not taking care of his responsibilities around the house. They had a terrible argument and Hope was in an angry rage, so she kicked him out of the house. She realized she could never have Brad and that she had made so many mistakes in her life, and she felt so hopeless.

Hope couldn't take anymore heartache, so she opened the bottle of pills sitting on the bedside table, and swallowed every last one of them down with a glass of water. She then lay down on the bed, and cried until she could not feel her face anymore. Feeling thankful that she was going to die, she closed her eyes, and David burst into the bedroom. Hope tried to get up but couldn't move. He had realized what she was going to do and had called 911. The ambulance was outside, and they were coming in after her. She was clinging to death while David was trying to save her. As they loaded her into the ambulance she could only utter the words "just let me die, I want to die".

She would go in and out of consciousness not realizing where she was and finally waking up in the psychiatric ward at the city hospital, surrounded by strangers. She was terrified! These people were drooling and screaming! They were incoherent! She did not belong here, and had to pull herself together and get out of here! And so she did!

When they finally allowed her use the phone, Hope called Charity. She told her to call the therapist, and tell him too get her out of there, and into his office as soon as he possibly could. Her therapist did not hide the fact that he was very fond of Hope, and went to work immediately to get her out of the hospital.

She was in his office that day, and he took responsibility for her. With a lot of counseling and persuasion, Hope pulled heself together and she packed up some of the things Brad had given her, took them to the home he shared with his wife, and left them on his front porch along with a goodbye letter. The letter explained that the five-year affair was over, and that she was returning some things, but keeping the jewelry, along with the money, for services rendered.

She felt that she had her power back. She was in control of her life again, something she had not felt in a long time, and wanted a new start. Hope turned in her notice at the plant, and explained the entire affair to the plant manager. The manager asked her to stay on as a supervisor. He wanted to fire Brad, but Hope would not have it that way. She explained that he was an old man, and close to retirement, but that she was still young, and could move on to find other work. Always looking out for someone else. So at the age of thirty nine she started over.

Chapter 20

HIS NAME WAS JOSH

HOPE GOT A job at a local factory, and the wages were very good. Many people tried to get a job there. but few were lucky enough to get hired. The work was hard, but she was no stranger to hard work, and was working alongside a lot of men, which was nothing she couldn't handle. The twelve-hour long night shifts weren't easy, and sleeping during the day was difficult. Hope was often in a bad mood ,which affected the relationship with her daughters. She would come home from work and find things in disarray, and get angry at the girls. They argued a lot, and it got so bad that they moved in with John, and it really hurt Hope, because she loved them more than life itself. John had never loved them the way she did, and he never would. This was the ultimate betrayal, and nothing had ever hurt her this bad in her entire life. The pain was so bad that work became her focus. She worked all the hours the plant would let her work. She was trying not to think about the girls living with John.

Hope could give sarcasm back to people just as good as it was given to her. When the men got nasty with her, she gave it right back. They tried her patience, but Hope won their respect. One man, in particular, tried her patience often, and one night when she was having a bad night, upset over her girls moving out of the house and into the house with John, she started crying when he yelled at her for messing up on her job. Hope ran away from her job, out onto the back dock, and he followed her.

He tried to console her, but there was no stopping her tears. As he apologized and consosled her, she saw a different side of him.Hope returned to her job, still crying, and they became friends at that moment. Of course, he was married and not happy! How many times had she heard that! His name was Josh.

Josh was Italian,and with quite a temper. He had dark skin and black hair, and was very handsome, but usually angry. Everyone knew he hated his wife. He worked ninety hours plus a week to pay his bills, and Hope worked every hour she could in order to keep her mind off of the girls. Within days he was telling Hope he loved her, and she asked him not to say that, because she was tired of being told that, and then being let down.

One day he showed up at her house, and they ended up in bed together. Is this not where it always starts, and ends? Just another painful end to another broken heart. Would Hope ever learn what love really was? So it was understood that she would not expect anything from Josh, and he should expect nothing from her. But Hope had underestimated this man.

Josh left his wife and moved in with his parents soon after the moment they were together, but he stayed with Hope most of the time. He was a drinker, but Hope didn't mind that at all, in fact, she started drinking too, and they had lots of fun together. Josh divorced his wife, and they were married as soon as his divorce was final.

At the age of forty-three, Hope was never as happy as she was at that moment in her life! His family adored her, and they treated her and her girls wonderfully! They were influential in the community and reasonably well off. She was finally part of a real family. Josh had a teenage son, but his son did not approve of Hope, or this marriage, and he did everything in his power to undermine the relationship, but Josh was determined to make this marriage work. Hope felt safe in love at last, and she let her guard down. She completely let go and lived life to the fullest for the first time ever. Her life was wonderful!

Charity was dating a guy and called and said she was pregnant. She was crying, but Hope comforted her and said it would be okay. Charity would marry the Father of her baby. His name was Luke. He was only two years older than Charity. His family had moved here from the mid-west and he was a handsome young man, who would turn out to be a wonderful Father and Husband, as well as a perfect son-in-law.

Hope would give Charity a beautiful wedding. She herself had only gotten married at a preachers home and courthouses. Tracy had two little girls by this time, and Rob had a little girl as well. They would all be a part of Charity's wedding, so they all came to stay at Hope's on the day before the wedding. When they were getting ready for the rehearsal, some dark secrets would be reaveled.

While Hope was trying to give Rob's daughter a bath, and make sure her hair was washed, she began to panic and hide her private parts. She became so upset that Hope suspected she had been molested. She had Tracy come into the bathroom to question her. They found her bottom very red and raw. After questioning her, they determined she had been molested, and they were pretty sure they knew by whom.

Tracy admitted that she had also been molested by her own dad as well, on many occasions. Hope was completely shocked, and then Joy joined in the conversation, and told things that were done to her that were to hard to comprehend! How could all this be happening now? On the eve of Charity's wedding day! One of the happiest days of Hope and Charity's lives. A new beginning for them all. Hope had finally found her happiness in life, and now it was as though things were coming apart all around her, and in her own home. She had to take control of this mess, so she did. Hope told them this would not interfere with her daughters big day. Bob was not here and would not be allowed around any of the children before, during, or after the wedding, and that as soon as everyone had left after the wedding was over, they would meet at Hope's and decide what to do about Bob.

After the reception was over and the couple took off for the honeymoon, all the guests left, and the family departed for home except for the married couple. Hope held a family meeting and told Rob about everything. Tracy and Joy told their part, and it was decided that Hope would be the one to call the police to report Bob. And so she did. By that evening Bob was calling Hope and begging her to get him out of jail. Hope, having anticipated just that, had purchased a recorder and hooked it up to her phone. She was taping the conversation. She offered to help him but said that if he had done nothing, then he had nothing to worry about. And unless he was willing to confess to having done something that she could not help him. So reluctantly he confessed. BAM!~She had him! She was nothing, if not smart! Men had taught her to be smart! She had learned from the best! Now maybe her mother would believe her. This would go to court, and they may all get to tell their stories. But no, Hope got to tell her story and Tracy hers. Robs little girl told her story, but Joy never got to tell hers.

Mother did not believe anything that was said and separated herself from all her children. He was arrested, and in court Mother sat there and rolled her eyes at Hope as she told her story, accusing all of them of being jealous of her and Bob. She claimed they only wanted to put him away in order have her to themselves. So that is how it was while he served two of the fifteen years he was sentenced to in prison. She would have nothing to do with her children until he was released.

Bob was raped by another inmate while there, and had to be placed in another part of the prison to prevent it from happening to him again. Hope found out later that he had molested several little girls in the trailer parks where they had lived. Bob called Mother every day because he was afraid she would talk to her children, believe them, and leave him. But he had nothing to worry about, because she would never leave him for her children, even though he had cheated on her, and she had cheated on him. They would be together until one of them died, and that was crystal clear.

Hope did reach out and try to help her Mother several times, upon hearing that she had no heat or food, but Mother rejected her help, saying that Hope just wanted her to leave Bob. Hope explained that when Bob was released, she was free to go back with him, but it was clear that Mother would only have a relationship with her children if Bob were involved.

Chapter 21

HER FIRST GRANDCHILD

HOPE HAD HER first Grandchild. It was a boy, and his name was Jake. She was right by Charity's side during his birth. Her heart had never been so filled with love! Life was so good! Hope spent every minute with possible with her Grandson! She sang to him, read to him, played Cowboys and Indians, race cars and anything else he wanted to do. She spent tons of money on him, and he would want for nothing. Her life was super perfect!

She and Josh traveled together, and took her children on lavish vacations. Their only problem was Josh's son. He hated Hope and said horrible things about her. She did everything she could to make him like her, but he never would.

Charity got pregnant again seven years later, but she was so sick this time. And there was something wrong with the baby. The months would drag by, and when the baby was born she was beautiful, but she was very sick. She lived only nine days. Her name was Tessa, and she looked perfect, but she did not make it. Hope hated that her instincts had been right. Faith was very angry at Hope, saying that she should have been more positive. There was a lot of tension and hard feelings going on at that time from Faith, but Hope stepped in and did everything possible to help her Charity.

Josh drove to the hospital and picked Tessa up in a little coffin and brought her to the funeral home, where the arrangements were made. It was the day before Christmas Eve when little Tessa was laid to rest in the cemetery, one mile from Hope's home. It was so cold that day, and it was snowing. Hope allowed her mother to attend the funeral, and instructed everyone to be civil for Charity's sake, or else. This day was all about Charity and her baby. It was about nothing else, and if anyone took advantage of this day for any other reason, they would answer to her. Joy, Hope, and her Mother became close on this day. Little Tessa's life was not in vain. This tragic event would change Hope's life forever. Hope was strong that day because she had to be.

Tessa's death took a toll on Charity. She was very depressed, and so was Hope. Hope lay in the floor cying, thinking that Tessa's grave wasn't dug deep enough and that stray dogs could somehow dig up her grave. She was tormented by these horrible thoughts. She stopped drinking and her life was never the same, and neither was her relationship with Faith. Hope became unable to work and had to file for disability. She didn't even have to go to court, but was awarded her disability the year after Tessa's death. She was fifty years old.

Chapter 22

RECONCILIATION

JOSH HAD A temper and from time to time he would lose it, but it didn't seem like much of a problem until one day when he was cutting the grass, and he started yelling at Hope to bring him his gun. He had done this before and she talked him out of it, but this day he was especially angry. The neighbors' dog was always coming into the yard. It had never done anything to Josh, but there had been something knocking over and getting into the garbage. They weren't sure whose dog it was, but Josh was determined that one day he was going to kill that dog. There were many times when he would yell at Hope to get his gun, but she would talk him out of killing the yellow lab. One day in particular Hope was in a bad place, and when he was angrily shouting for her to get his gun, she didn't try talking him down. She got his gun, took it to him, and could not believe it when she heard the gunshot.

He had actually killed the dog! One of the neighbors immediately came over, and together they took the body away. When the owner of the dog came home that day, the neighbor who had helped Josh dispose of the body, told him what had happened, and all hell broke loose at Hope's house. There were death threats to Hope and Josh, the windows were broken and other things destroyed before the police could get there. Hope was curled up in her home in a corner crying, reliving memories of her childhood, from her angry father and his outrages! She had lived here with her daughters, in this home she bought for them, for over thirteen years, and knew that she was going to have to sell it and move. All because Josh had done this terrible thing.

Josh was arrested and taken to jail, and she bailed him out. The matter went to court and Josh was fined over twenty-five hundred dollars for the life of the dog and her unborn puppies. Hope sold her home, and they bought ten acres of land in the country where they lived in a motor home while they built a home. Hope would try to make the best of this bad situation and she designed her new home. A Beautiful home! A new start!

Josh was excited about the new home construction, and it went well. The home was beautiful. Neither he nor Hope had ever had such a lovely home before. They furnished it with beautiful things. Since Tessa's death Hope had confessed all of her sins to God, begged Him to forgive her, and surrendered her life to Him. She started looking for a Church and found one. Josh would not go with her at first and he was not happy with her going either but he eventually started going with her to Church and their lives changed completely. For the first time in a long time, Hope felt that her life could be complete. She played the piano, and sang in Church, while Josh participated in every activity he could. Hope was strong, and very determined to make this marriage work.

Josh's mother passed away, and it was a sad time for them both. His dad was lost without her, and was showing signs of dementia. Josh was struggling with the loss of his mother and he loved his dad so much. It was very hard to see his dad slipping away. At this time Josh started to help his sister's take care of his dad , and that is when Josh began to slip away. His relationship with his sisters started to suffer, and they would argue about things concerning his dad's finances. He even became paranoid that his older sister was taking money from his Dad. It was as though he hated his two sisters, which he used to be so close with at one time. The family that was once strong, was coming apart. Josh was coming apart.

Hope was often sad, for what seemed like no reason at all, but had seen so much sadness in her life that perhaps it was normal to feel this way. She had stopped taking her anti-depressants, as she often did, but Josh seemed determined to cheer her up, so one day he persuaded her to go on an errand with him.

They pulled up to a pet store, and he wanted her to go inside with him. She was hesitant because she did not like reptiles, and refused to go inside. He went inside, and came out with the most beautiful puppy in the world. Her heart melted! Josh asked her if she would like to have the puppy, and she cried tears of joy, while blurting out the answer "yes"! Hope named her after her favorite movie character, Scarlett, and she became a part of the family that day. Scarlett was a bright light for Hope, and things seemed good for a while, but they wouldn't stay that way. Things never seemed to stay good for Hope.

Because of the hard labor jobs they had done at the factory, they suffered much physical pain, and it had gotten so bad they sought out a pain relief clinic in a nearby town. They were both given pain medications, anxiety pills, and steroid injections to help alleviate the pain. This would lead them down a path of ultimate doom that would tear them apart. The medication helped the pain so much that Josh felt better than he had in years. He kept five out of the ten acres of grass cut each week in the summer. He became very active, and Hope felt better so she was always cooking. The house was clean all the time. But she noticed that he was not taking his medicine correctly.

One day, when going to his Dad's after Church, Josh asked her to tune the radio to a sports station. He became frustrated with her because she couldn't find it, took his eyes off the road, and started trying to find it himself. He was driving very fast, so when Hope looked up and saw a van stopped in front of them she screamed. Josh slammed on the brakes, but it was too late. They crashed into the van. The windshield was broken into so many pieces, and fell into the car onto them. The airbags were activated, and both of them plunged forward into the airbags. Smoke was coming into the car. Hope was confused but she managed to get out of the car and onto the side of the highway, into the grass. She lay on the grass, but Josh insisted that she get up. When she refused he became angry with her, so she stood up in order to appease him. Rescue squads, and ambulances came and took all the injured to the hospital. Josh and Hope were carefully examined and dismissed. Miraculously, the car was not totaled, but was towed to a shop, where it was repaired, but it was several months before it was finished.

Due to the fact that Hope had degenerative disc disease and spinal stenosis, she had to have another back surgery. This was number three and the worst one yet. She had already had two neck surgeries. During the second one she had lost a vocal cord, and had not spoken one word for seven months. Thankfully her vocal cord was not harmed in this surgery.

When she left the hospital from her surgery she was in a lot of pain. Josh had to do something for his Dad so instead of taking her home he drove to his Dad's and picked him up and ran all the errands for him with Hope in the car. By the time she got home, she was really in a lot of pain but she didn't complain.

Within days she felt as though there were rocks inside of her back, and had been sewn up inside her. Her incision was leaking yellow fluid, and the papers read that if this happened, get to the emergency room, or at least call her physician. She expressed these feelings with Josh, and he became argumentative with her. He had been changing her bandages, and argued that it looked fine to him, that she was overreacting. When she asked him to take another look, he jerked her arm, pulling her roughly down the hall to the bathroom mirror. He jerked the bandage off, and exclaimed, "see, it looks fine". But it didn't, and it hurt like hell. She cried, telling him he should not handle her roughly like that anymore or she would call the police. This made Josh very angry, and she could see that, so she went to the other bedroom to sleep.

Within minutes the doorbell rang, and the police were in her room. Josh had called the police. He told them she was bipolar, and even showed them her medicine. They asked her if he had hurt her, and if she was scared of him. She told them he had gotten rough with her. They informed Hope they would be taking her out of the house and not him! NOT HIM! Not knowing where they would take her, and afraid it would be to a mental hospital,she changed her story, telling them everything would be fine and that she had overreacted, and was not afraid. They finally went away. How could he have done that to her? The next morning Hope had a temperature of 102.8 and her incision was red. When she ventured out of the bedroom Josh tried to apologize. and realized she was sick. He took her to the emergency room, they admitted her immediately and did emergency surgery on her back. It was opened up, washed in antibiotics, then closed up again. When she woke they informed her that she had a severe staph infection, and her organs were shutting down. They told her to call her family in right away, and that they would do everything they could to save her life, but at this point were not sure they could. The blood disease specialist was brought in and would be trying a combination of the six strongest antibiotics available, intravenously, 24/7 to try and rid her from the infection. But Hope didn't care, and wanted to die. The love of her life had changed on her. He had become another person and she was tired. She didn't feel strong anymore, and didn't want to try, or hope anymore. But she would because her name was Hope.

Her family came to see her. Even her mother. By this time Bob had gotten out of prison. He had only served two of the fifteen years he had been sentenced. They surrounded her with love, hugs, and kisses. Prayers went up that day. Kind, encouraging, and beautiful words were spoken from and to each other that day. Apologizes were made and accepted that day too. It was a day of reconciliation, and Hope's family were somehow brought closer that day.

Hope went home from the hospital after eight days with a PICC line in her arm, that was surgically placed inside of her which she would be wearing for months to come. It would pump antibiotics into her body 24/7. Josh would be in charge of changing the bags out every 24 hours, He felt really bad about the way he had treated Hope, and was really trying to make it up to her. But somehow she could not forget about the hurtful things he had done. She could forgive, but never forget when men hurt her. Hurt me once shame on you, hurt me twice shame on me! She did recover, but not without suffering, and was left so weak from all the antibiotics with their side affects. Everything she ate came right out. She could hardly walk and had lost forty-five pounds, but she beat it.

Chapter 23

WOULD ANYONE
EVER LOVE HER?

HOPE NEVER REGAINED her strength, and had to ask Josh to help her around the house. Josh seemed to drift away emotionally. He stayed up late at night, long after she went to bed, and sleep late the next day. He would try and hide his phone conversations from Hope, and hang up quickly when she came into the room. She became suspicious, and hid behind the door once, in order to find out who he was talking to, and it came as no shock to find out it was the woman he had been involved with before marrying his ex-wife. This is the woman Josh had claimed to love, but she wouldn't marry him because of his drinking problem. In her heart she knew that he still loved this woman, and would never love anyone quite as much as he had ever loved her. Josh heard that she was about to get married, and he told her they had unfinished business. Hope waited until he hung the phone up, told Josh she had been listening, and that if he felt he had unfinished business with her that he should finish it, He was in shock, but Hope was dead serious. He called this woman several times, but she did not want him. Hope gave him every chance to have his wish because she thought this would help him get over that woman, and that she had done the right thing, when in reality, her rejection had sent Josh into an ever darker place.

His moods alternated between violent anger and dark depression, and Hope didn't know how to help him. Somehow during one of their many arguments, Josh made Hope leave. She packed a bag and headed to her Mother's in Georgia, and was determined never to go back to him. She bought her a cell phone and began to believe that it was finally over. She awoke the next morning to the sound of the phone ringing at her Mothers. It was Josh calling, and he told her that if she wasn't home in one hour that he would burn the god***m house to the ground. She begged him to give her some time, but he was angry and adamant. Hope had no choice but to gather her things together quickly and drive as fast as she could to get home. She prayed all the way there that her home would be standing when she arrived. Thank God it was. Hope never thought of these incidents as abuse because they had not been physical. Josh had never hit her ,kicked her, or thrown her around like a rag doll as her father had done. Little did she know this was a precursor to what was to come.

Josh was slowly slipping away, so Hope planned short day trips, trying to distract Josh from thinking about her, but he couldn't even stay awake enough to drive back home. She had to drive back while he slept. Once they took a weekend trip to the beach, and he slept the entire weekend in the room. There was very little intimacy any- more, and when there was it ended in disappointment for both of them. He had begun trying to make Scarlett to come and sit with him, and would not allow her to sit with Hope when they were watching television.

One day when he got angry, he threw his wallet at her, hit her right hip and injured her, and she limped from that day forward. Hope cried and held Scarlett, and couldn't understand how anyone could be so cruel to such an innocent little animal. She loved Scarlett with her whole heart and he was as cruel as her Dad, and she saw him in a different way, as she had often times before. He had mentioned that he wanted to start drinking again and she was troubled by this confession. After all this time what would make him want to resort to drinking? Why this sudden urge to become the person he used to be? She was so confused as to what was going on with him.

He was spending a lot of time with his Dad who had gone into a facility for the elderly with dementia. This had made him very sad, and of course she understood that. She didn't go with him enough to see his Dad, and later on would regret that. She knew she was drifting away from him too, and that the marriage was falling apart, but couldn't leave. Hope had come to depend on Josh, and didn't feel as though she could make it financially anymore on her own. The house payment was totally out of her ability to pay. She felt hopeless. How had she allowed her life to come to this? What had happened to her marriage? Surely it should be better than this. But she was determined to stay in this marriage if it killed her! Little did she know how close it would come to doing just that.

Hope decided that she wanted another car. She was tired of the constant reminder of the wreck he had in the car they were driving. It was a reminder that Josh had been irresponsible and she insisted they buy a new car. Josh was reluctant but he gave in and they bought a brand new car.

While driving home from Church on a dark country road, late one night Josh ran into a ditch. The car was stuck in the ditch on the passenger side where Hope was sitting. She didn't understand why he had run into the ditch. He started trying to back out of it by backing up, then pulling forward, crashing into the ditch each time he pulled forward, and slamming her into the side of the ditch. She begged him to stop, trying to reason with him, he finally stopped and called for help. A wrecker came and towed the car to a nearby body shop and they walked to their home. Hope was confused and Josh seemed disoriented. What was wrong with him? The pain medicine! They had to drive a rental car once again while the car was in the shop.

They had become total strangers, and the silence was almost deafening. There seemed to be no good days anymore. Josh sat in front of the television all of the time. and Hope busied herself with the housework and read the Bible hoping to find comfort in God's Word. But the loneliness finally got the best of her and soon Hope thought about the man she had once loved, long ago. She began to think of Paul. She remembered the love she had felt for him, wondering if he ever thought of her. and what could have been if only he had left his wife for her. She needed to feel loved again, and couldn't resist the urge to call him so she did.

She knew this was wrong but the need to feel loved overcame her conscience. His wife answered the phone, and she pretended to be a salesperson for some random company, trying to sell something, and was told no immediately. She thanked her and hung up the phone, waited for a few minutes and called back. He answered the phone, and her heart lept in her body just to hear his voice. She asked him if he remembered a woman from the year nineteen eighty-one. He hesitated for a moment, and then said no. She told him to think really hard but he said he didn't think so. Maybe he did, but had to say those words because she was listening, or maybe he really did not remember. Her heart was sad as she hung up the phone. She felt a little guilty, but also felt as though no one in the whole world cared. Would anyone ever love her? Was her life really over?

What would she do, and why had her life come to such a sad end? Living without the love of a man would feel empty, and hopeless. She knew that God loved her, but needed to hear that she was important and loved, and needed to feel loving arms around her sometimes. Need was a word that Hope hated, but she had become needy,weak, and had let her guard down, She totally trusted Josh, and because of that, was not strong anymore. Oh God, how could she have let this happen? Fifty-nine years old now, and afraid that she would have to start all over again, fat, unattractive, unemployed, and on disability. She could never afford to keep this home, because the mortgage payments were almost as much as the amount of her monthly check. With nowhere to go, how would she live? So many questions in her mind, and so little solutions. She would stay as long as she could, and try to make it work.

Josh started getting angry at the people at Church, talking bad about them, complaining that they didn't like him, and he stopped going to Church with Hope. Everyone asked why he was not coming, but Hope didn't have an answer for them. The pastor sat with her one night, and talked with her. He knew something was wrong. He asked if he could come to their home to visit with Josh, and she said yes. When she got home and told Josh that the pastor was coming to visit he went into a rage. He told her that if the pastor came to their home he would cut him with a knife until his guts gushed out, or shoot and kill him. That if he stepped foot on the property he would be within his rights to kill him, because he would be trespassing. Hope could not believe what she had just heard him say, but she knew he was capable of doing just that. She was taken back to her childhood days when her Dad would pull knives and guns on her Mother. It was terrifying! She ran into the other room to call the pastor and warn him. Josh picked up the other phone, and began to tell the pastor the same thing he had told her. This night had become a total nightmare for Hope. They had words and he shoved her up against the wall, and with his hands on her neck, he began to choke her. He told her he could break her neck like snapping a toothpick into half. He was a very strong man. That was one of the things she loved about him, but not when he was violent.

Hope was not afraid at that moment, because she knew that if he killed her that her pain and sadness would finally be over, and that gave her peace. He let go of her and she went to the other bedroom and stayed that nigt, but sleep didn't come easy. She lay there and thought of their friends that had gone on vacation with them a few years back. Carrie was a nurse, and Ted worked with them at their last job. They were a power couple, having lots of rental houses, and living in a beautiful home. They drank, and argued a lot, but always seemed to be happy. Recently, Ted had strangled Carrie while in a rage, and killed her. He put her in the trunk of her car. and drove her to a deserted place. She was found later that day. and he was arrested not long after that, and would be spending his life in prison. Could this be how it ends for her and Josh?

The next day there was total silence, but you could tell that Josh was very angry. Hope was working in the kitchen and he was sitting in the great room. The house was very open and they could see each other Suddenly Josh started shouting profanity, telling her to get the f**k out over and over. She just got the keys to the only vehicle they had at the time, the truck, and left. She was not really scared, she was just angry. So angry in fact that she went looking for a place to live.

She stayed gone for about two hours, and as she was pulling into the garage she didn't notice that he had run into it, and he started pounding on the passenger window, yelling profanity to get the "F" out and leave. She calmly got out of the truck and went into the house. He was sitting in the great room when she got inside. She didn't notice the gun in his hand as she sat down. He told her to leave, and she told him that this was her home too. Then he started waving the gun around and said: "old woman, you have thirty minutes to get your s**t together and get the h**l out before something bad happens, and you need to call your daughter". She told him she wasn't going to call her daughter, so he picked up the phone and called Charity and told her that she should come and get her Mother before something bad happened to her. Hope started gathering up some things in a plastic bag. Charity called her on her cell, and told her to get her things and start walking, that she would pick her up on the road and not to stay one minute longer than necessary, so Hope did just that.

When she left walking, the neighbor saw her going down the road, and started driving to pick her up. She had seen this happen before when he made her leave. About that time Charity pulled up as well, Hope got in her car, and they drove away. Josh's sister called her on her cell at this time and asked if she was okay. She couldn't understand how his sister knew about this, and asked her how she knew. She told Hope he had put it all on social media, and asked Hope to have him put in jail because she thought he would kill himself. Hope would not do that because she was afraid that he would get out of jail and come after her. Later on in life she would rethink that, and wish she had done differently. But you can't go back in time and do things over.

Hope felt like she had fallen into a dark hole, onto a hard rock, and was broken into a million pieces and couldn't be put back together again. Hopeless, that is how she felt, hopeless. But she still loved Josh, and would always be in love with him. He was the love of her life. What would life be without him? In her heart, she felt that Josh was a good man but that somehow he was broken and needed help. How could she still love him after all this? Hope didn't want their marriage to end. She wanted him to get better, and wanted them to get better. Was that even possible?

As Charity was driving to her home, Hope was crying with a broken heart, and Charity informed her that if she went back to Josh, that she and Faith would have nothing to do with her ever again. This was the final blow to Hope's heart. It was as though someone had taken a sword, and drove it through her chest, and she would die right there in that car. Hope actually wanted to die. The pain was so bad, so excruciating, that she thought her heart would stop beating. Now she would have to choose between Josh and her children.

How do you choose between the love of your life and your babies? Your Mother chose a man over you, and you understand all too well how that affects you for the rest of your life. Will you do that to your babies? NO! You would never choose a man over your own children. That pain never goes away and therefore you will bear the pain of losing the man you love with all your heart for as long as you live in order to spare your children the pain of their Mother choosing a man over her children. And that is what Hope chose to do that very moment. That was, without a doubt, the most painful moment of Hope's life, or so she thought. Little did she know that her pain would go on for a long time to come.

Chapter 24

HOPE HAD TO START OVER

HOPE STAYED WITH Charity, trying to get her mind straight, but she couldn't get it together. Josh was constantly calling her cell, and she would answer. He was begging her to come home, but she would tell him she couldn't right now. He came there one night banging on the door, calling for Hope, and Jake got really upset. He ran upstairs and grabbed his gun. This upset Hope so much, because she loved Jake more than anyone in her life and it was so sad to see him this way. He was too young to go through this, and should not be experiencing all this drama. Luke went outside and talked to Josh. He calmed him down, and told him to give Hope some time. Josh left, but he continued to call. Hope stopped answering his calls because her daughters insisted she stopped talking to him. Charity and Faith took control of the situation. They told Hope that she should get a lawyer, and she got the best lawyer in town. They took her to the appointment that day, and the lawyer suggested she get alimony, the house, the car and other things, but Hope said she didn't want anything but a divorce. The girls weren't having it that way at all, and explained to Hope that she had a home when Josh came along, and because of him she had to sell it and she deserved something from him. Hope settled for half the equity in the home, and most of the furniture but she wanted no alimony. She had always started over with little or nothing, but her girls wanted more for her this time.

She and the girls went there to pack up her things to move, and Josh was very angry. He sat there in the great room and glared at them while they packed. Hope hired some movers to come and get the furniture, and she went back alone one day to pack up her things in the kitchen and dining room. He started asking her what it would take to make her stay. She told him that if he would see a therapist and get well she would consider coming back. He said that if she would come back he would see a therapist, but not until she came back. There was no talking him into getting therapy unless she came home, and she would not come back until he could get well. But in her heart, she knew he would never get well, and knew she could not go back and choose him over her children. Hope would not do that even though she wanted to go back to him so much. That decision had already been made, and could not be changed. There was no going back now, He started getting angry, and she got scared that he would get the gun out again. so she got in a hurry, only to find out much later on that she had forgotten to pack some items belonging to her Grandmother that she would never see again. Things that meant so much to her. She was about to take Scarlett with her when he informed her that she could not have Scarlett. It broke Hope's heart to leave her puppy behind, but there was no arguing with Josh.

She stored her things in a mini-warehouse and proceeded with the divorce. Hope found a cute little home close to Charity and tried to settle into her new life. She found her a new Church and made some wonderful friends. One night Josh called and asked Hope to come and take him to the hospital because he thought he was having a heart attack. She told him to call 911, but he asked her to please come and take him to the emergency room, and she did. They told him he was just having an anxiety attack, but they would keep him overnight. He looked so sad and tired, but Hope had to act as though she didn't care. She could not take him back, and lose her family, so after more than seventeen years of marriage, Hope had to start over.

When Josh got out of the hospital his attitude changed. He had ordered him a new Mustang convertible, and showed it to Hope. His son was married now, and they had just had a baby. Josh took her to see his new granddaughter. Hope wanted to be with him, but she didn't want her girls to know. He had come by her house and gotten his old school annuals and some of his favorite CD's. They would have lunch together once in a while. He tried to get her to come back to him but she could not lose her daughters.

The time came when he no longer answered Hope's calls and she knew she had lost him. Hope soon discovered that Josh was dating someone. In fact, he was leaving Scarlett alone for an entire week, while he was staying at her house, and then they would come to his house and stay for a week. Her name was Ann.

She did not like pets, so Josh decided that he would give Scarlett back to Hope. But she had already gotten her another puppy. Apparently, he had gone out with Ann once when he was in high school, and while looking in the annual one night he came across her and decided to look her up. Her husband had died of cancer, so they hooked up. Josh found out that she had money, and lots of it. He needed money at that time because he had spent all that he had on the new car, and was struggling financially, so soon, they were living together in the house that Hope once shared with the love of her life. Josh brought Scarlett to Hope's house one day, with all her things, and left her there, without saying a word, and Scarlett was so traumatized that she had lost control of her bladder as well as her bowels.

It was killing Hope that Josh was moving on. She was terrified of think of life without him. She started calling him and he didn't answer her calls, until the one time he picked up and warned her that if continued to call that he was going to have her arrested for harassment. Oh God how her heart was torn into pieces! She could never have Josh back! He was gone, and she wanted to die! She was dead inside already. A shell of a woman, lost and drifting in a sea of sorrow and heartache, without hope, and drowning in her own tears. The pain was unbearable. She would rather be raped or murdered. Death was one thing she had never feared. But this was more that she could bear, and she was broken.

The fact that Josh already with someone else was killing Hope. There were days she did not get out of bed and nights when she lay prostate in the floor crying, praying, screaming, begging God to bring him back to her. She wished she could sleep all the time and dream that he was lying next to her in bed. Was there any hope that she would ever hold him in her arms again? How much could a heart take before it stopped beating? She questioned why he could move on so quickly. But then again, he was a man, and men seemed to be able to snap right back. Why had she, all of a sudden not unable to find someone else? That was a good question?

Chapter 25

NO ONE WOULD
HURT HER AGAIN

SINCE HOPE WAS back in a relationship with her mother, she started spending a few days and nights there. Mother had been diagnosed with dementia, and was soon placed in a nursing home. While visiting there one day, the conversation came up about a man that Joy used to date. Hope remembered a time when she had dinner at his apartment with the two of them. He was very handsome at the time, but Joy had been divorced then and had since gone back to her husband. Even though Joy had some bad things to say about him Hope was interestd. She would do anything to get Josh off her mind. The conversation ended but it stayed in Hope's mind.

When she returned home, Hope found him on social media, and reached out to him. The two of them connected, and began a friendship, but when Joy found out about it, she was extremely angry, and told him Hope was a drug addict. When Hope heard what Joy had said about her it was shocking at first, but then she became angry. How could she say that about her? Hope had never been a drug addict. Hope was so angry that she wanted revenge, and without a second thought she revealed secrets about Joy's past, as well as her own. He invited her to come and visit him in Louisiana, and she did. She stayed three days with him, but slept in the guest room alone. This was strictly retaliation against Joy, but when she was about to leave to go home, Hope kissed him goodbye and actually enjoyed the kiss.

He visited Hope a month later, and he slept on her sofa. By this time Joy had heard the news about the visits, and she had sent Hope some very hurtful and nasty letters, cutting Hope's heart into. Ugly things that hurt so much, but Hope said nothing back to her. Hope actually thought they could get past this. A few months later, Hope called Joy on her birthday to wish her well, only to be called horrible names and realized they may never be close again. Her husband Had been killed in a tragic automobile accident and Joy was having trouble getting over his death and the trouble they had during the years of their on again off again marriage.

Hope tried to apologize to Joy by sending cards, and calling, but she finally gave up. There seemed to irreparable damage, and this was something that would ultimately tear Hope's heart apart. This man became angry if Hope didn't answer the phone immediately when he called, and it didn't take long for her to realize that she wanted nothing more to do with him. Was she finally getting smart? She had lost her ability to hold down a full-time job, a precious Granddaughter, a husband who was the love of her life that she couldn't seem to get over, a home, a sister that she had been very protective of (who had become her enemy), and a family (even though they were messed up). What could be next? She was about to find out.

Faith was cold toward Hope, and stayed angry at her all the time. One Christmas she had even called and cursed Hope so bad that it devestated her and she cried all day on Christmas Day. It seemed as though Hope could do nothing right. Faith started cursing Hope for any little thing she thought was wrong, and would make ugly comments that hurt Hope. At Christmas gatherings, Faith would make fun of Hope. Once Hope posted a picture of her small family at Christmas time on social media. When Faith found out, she called and cursed Hope so terribly the next day, that she cried all day long. Her heart was so broken, and her Christmas was ruined. Hope knew that Faith was also bipolar, just as she and Charity were, but Faith was off her medicine, and would not go back on it. Knowing this didn't make Hope feel any better about the abuse coming from her daughter, because she was losing Faith too. Even though she had chosen her children over Josh, she was losing one of them anyway. Did Faith not know what Hope had given up for her? Didn't she realize how much Hope loved her? Hope was so depressed that she couldn't cope with everyday life, and got rid of her pets, not being able to care for them or herself anymore. Charity took one and gave the other to Faith, which only increased her anger and hatred.

Hope found out that Faith was having fertility treatments in order to have a baby. They had been trying for years with no results, but she had finally gotten pregnant. Hope only knew because Charity told her. Faith was having nothing to do with Hope, no matter how hard Hope had tried. When the baby was born, Hope begged see the baby. He was premature, weighing only two pounds, but Faith refused to let her see him. Hope was determined to see that baby boy and she went anyway. Faith was furious, and would not even look at Hope. His name was Reed, and he had to stay in the hospital for three months. Faith did not leave the entire time he was in the hospital. Hope got to see and touch him once, and when he came home she was allowed to see him only when Faith was not at home, and her Mother-in-law was there keeping him. This hurt Home more that she could bear, and was starting to take a toll on her mental health. She was losing weight at an alarming rate.

Hope had financial problems, and had started sitting with the elderly. She was sitting with a lady at night, and would go visit the baby in the morning after work. She got to hold him and feed him, but her depression was getting worse and worse. She had a bipolar episode, and had traded her car in for a new Camaro, making her financial situation worse, which made her depression worse. Hope had managed to get off all the pain medication, but had not thrown it away, and her sciatic nerve pain had come back with a vengeance. She had just had another back surgery, but it gave her no relief. She was beginning to feel that she had no reason to live, and had started thinking that both she and her family would be better off dead. Hope had some great life insurance, and Charity struggled financially, so if she were dead, Charity could get out of debt. She had changed her Last Will and Testament and was leaving Charity everything, since it was clear that Faith wanted nothing to do with her. How much more could she lose without losing herself? Hope felt there was only one way out, and that was to take her life, and she would do just that. No one would hurt her again.

Hope was tired of being hurt, and losing the people she loved. It was time to put an end to the pain she had suffered all of her life. Hope quit her job sitting with the lady at night, and carefully planned her suicide, and wrote down the details for her memorial service down to the very last detail, including every song that was to be played, the Pastor at her Church that was to speak, and where her ashes were to be scattered. She wrote letters to Faith, Charity, Jake, and Reed; laid all the pills out on her bed, and put her pajamas on.

Hope carefully placed the fentanyl patches all over her body, and swallowed the pills down with a glass of water. She then created a text, and after some time had passed, sent it to Charity, telling her how much she loved her, that soon Charity's financial problems would be over, and that just in case anything were to ever happen to Hope she could find all of the information in a lock box in the hall closet. Then Hope closed her eyes and slept, believing in her heart that her troubles were finally over, but she was wrong.

Hope had been in a hallucinogenic state for over two weeks. She thought the staff was trying to kill her, had become very combative, and resisted everyone who was taking care of her. She was on a ventilator, not able to breathe on her own, and a feeding tube unable to swallow. Weeks later Hope awoke to a voice in the hospital saying she was alive. It mad her so angry she cursed! Damn it! They asked why she was angry, and she said that she wanted to die. Hope was in a very bad place, and would forever suffer for what she had done. Her life would never be the same again. She would never sing, talk, or even breathe normally again, and vividly remembered that the

Bible read, we always reap what we sow. She would find these words to be very true.

Charity had been coming every day to see her. Her Sunday School Teacher had been coming every day as well. Faith had only come once and was not very friendly to her friends who were there. Jake had even come to see her after she had woke up. She graduated from the ventilator that was breathing for her to a tracheotomy. She began to talk, but not very well. After a week they removed the trach but she was still unable to swallow. Her feeding tube would come loose at night and leak all over her bed. She would ring for the nurses but they wouldn't come, so she lay in a wet bed and was without nutrition until someone would come in and find her in this mess.

Hope was in the hospital for over a month. She couldn't be dismissed until she could pass a swallowing test to see if she could eat and drink. If she could not pass the test, she would have to have a tube in her stomach, and feed herself through the tube. Hope had given up, and decided to get the tube, and felt as hopeless as she had ever felt in her life. Her Church held a special prayer vigil, with twelve people, hand in hand, the night before she was to have the final swallowing test, and the next morning, she passed the test. God had truly come through for her. Hope finally realized that God did love her, and that she had shortchanged Him all of her life. God cared about her, and she had counted on everyone but Him, but not anymore. Now she would count on Him, because He was the only one trustworthy, and whose word is true. She would would need physical therapy every day for two months, and have to learn to walk, talk and breathe again.

Charity took Hope home from the hospital that day. She told her it hurt very badly that Hope had done this, and that if it ever happened again that she would not stand by her. Hope understood that she had really hurt her daughter, and she told her that she would never, ever do it again, and that she was very sorry. She told Charity how much she loved and appreciated how she had stood by her, and called 911 that day. Hope's life changed that day, but it wasn't easy.

Even though she wanted to die because of all the people she had lost in her life, and the things she had suffered, Hope was determined to live for God, and try to make a better life for herself, a life not dependent on the love of a man. She would be strong again. She had hope again.

But things would not be easy and she did not realize the struggle that was ahead of her. The one thing she did know is that God promised that He would never leave or forsake her and she must hold to that promise!

Look for more about Hope's recovery and struggles to come in an upcoming book!

CPSIA information can be obtained
at www.ICGtesting.com
Printed in the USA
BVHW082005040319
541724BV00001B/261/P